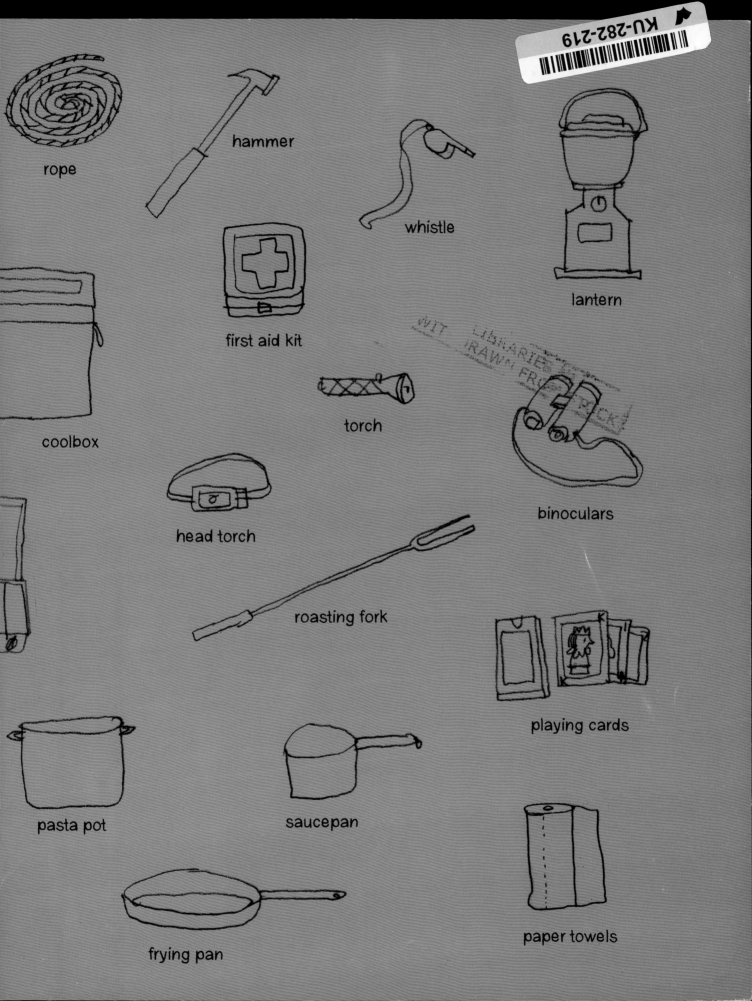

rope

hammer

whistle

lantern

first aid kit

coolbox

torch

binoculars

head torch

roasting fork

playing cards

pasta pot

saucepan

frying pan

paper towels

This book is dedicated with love to
Anna, Curren, Eliza, Than, and their parents.
Thank you for all the unforgettable camping
memories already made, and those yet to come.

First published 2020 by Walker Books Ltd
87 Vauxhall Walk, London SE11 5HJ

2 4 6 8 10 9 7 5 3 1

© 2020 Jennifer K. Mann

The right of Jennifer K. Mann to be identified as author and illustrator of this work has
been asserted by her in accordance with the Copyright, Designs and Patents Act 1988

This book has been typeset in Archer and AnkeSans

Printed in China

British Library Cataloguing in Publication Data: a catalogue record for this book is
available from the British Library

ISBN 978-1-4063-9350-7

www.walker.co.uk

THE CAMPING TRIP

Jennifer K. Mann

WALKER BOOKS
AND SUBSIDIARIES
LONDON • BOSTON • SYDNEY • AUCKLAND

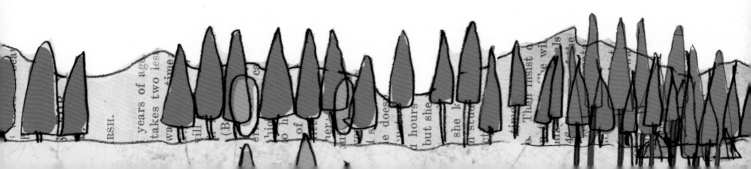

MY AUNT JACKIE invited me to go camping with her and my cousin Samantha this weekend, and my dad said yes!

I've never been camping before, but I know I will love it.

I got a sleeping bag ...

and a new torch!

And Dad and I made some snacks, just for camping.

Aunt Jackie sent a list of things to pack:

hat

trainers

torch

water bottle

backpack

pyjamas

towel

camera

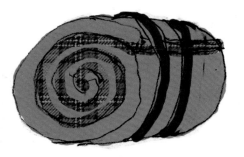

sleeping bag

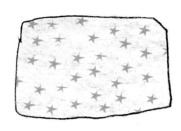

pillow

suncream

underwear

swimming costume

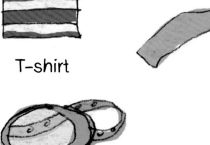

shorts

Foxy

sunglasses

plasters

T-shirt

jumper

swim mask

socks

comic books

whistle

snacks

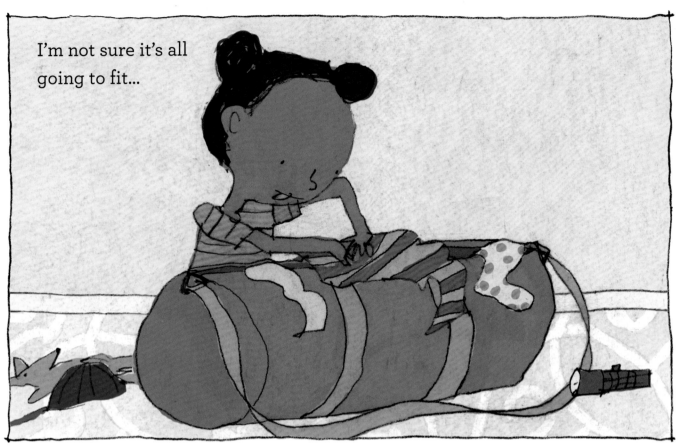

I'm not sure it's all going to fit...

I'm ready!

Then I wait and wait.

It's a long drive to Cedar Tree Campsite.

We look at comic books.

We play cat's cradle.

We stare out the window.

We sing along with the radio.

Finally, we're here!

It's so quiet. And big.
It smells like trees, and fire,
and dirt.

You need a lot of stuff to go camping, so it takes a long time to unpack.

Samantha and I decide to set up the tent. I build forts all the time at home, so this should be easy.

It's not one bit easy.

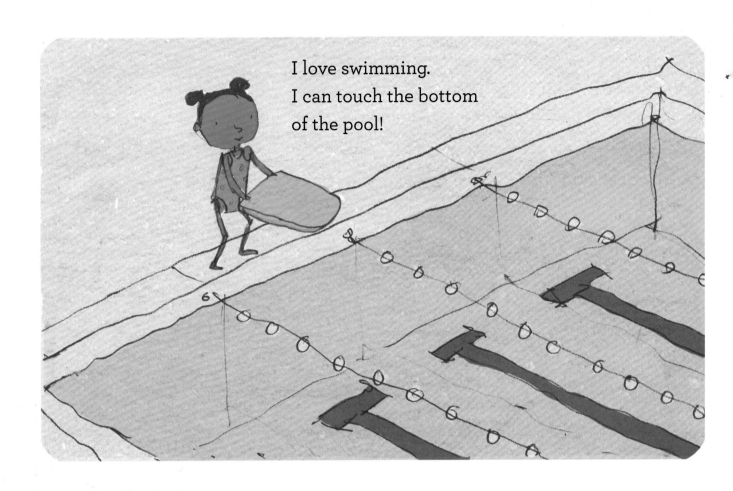

I love swimming.
I can touch the bottom
of the pool!

There are fish in here!

Don't worry, Ernestine!

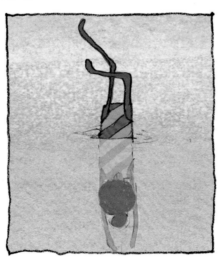

The fish won't bite you, promise.

That's OK. I'll just watch you swim.

When Samantha is finally done swimming, we eat lunch.

My dad says hiking is just walking – but in nature instead of in the city – and I walk to school every day.

Here's what I need
to go hiking:

backpack
hat
sunglasses
whistle
camera
water bottle
suncream
granola bar
snacks
apple
raisins and peanuts
leftover crisps
cheese sticks
crackers
biscuits
plasters
Foxy

There are a lot more hills here
than on my way to school.

My feet are tired already.

Maybe I brought too much stuff.

I think I need a water break.

When we finally stop, I eat a lot so my backpack will be lighter on the way back!

It's way easier to hike downhill.

When we get back to the campsite, Samantha and I set up the campfire.

Tofu hot dogs are *not* my favourite.

But I'm really hungry.

This broccoli is good!

Wait till you try s'mores. They're scrumptious!

This is what you need for s'mores:

marshmallow

biscuits

chocolate

a marshmallow–roasting fork

First you roast your marshmallow over a campfire.

Then you make a sandwich.

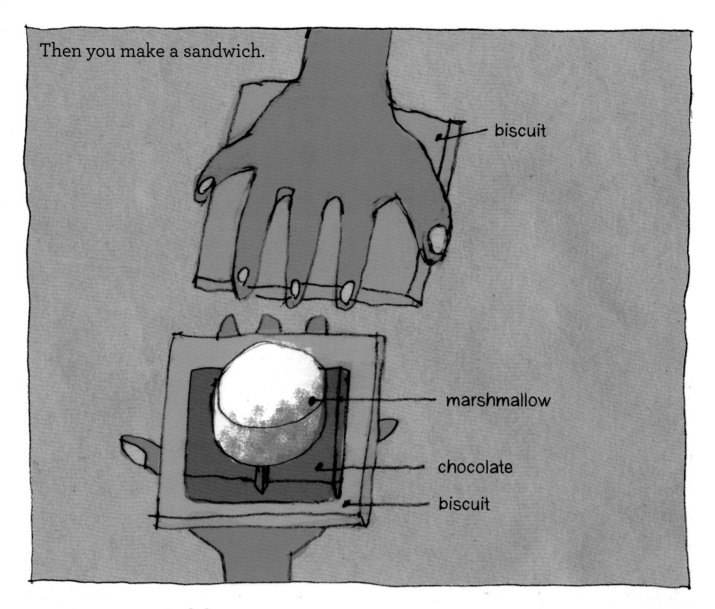

biscuit

marshmallow

chocolate

biscuit

And then you eat it. S'mores *are* scrumptious!

Before we know it, night is all around us.

I crawl into my sleeping bag, and we read with light from
Aunt Jackie's lantern until she says it's time to sleep.

Two seconds later, Aunt Jackie and Samantha are snoring. But I can't sleep.

I'm boiling.

I need to get my socks off!

Where's my water bottle?

Where is Foxy?

I'm freezing.

Is anyone else awake?

Is Dad awake?

Aunt Jackie lets me use her phone, but there is no signal.

It's really dark.

When I wake up in the morning,
the tent is warm and bright.

Aunt Jackie and Samantha
are already eating breakfast.

These are the best
pancakes ever!

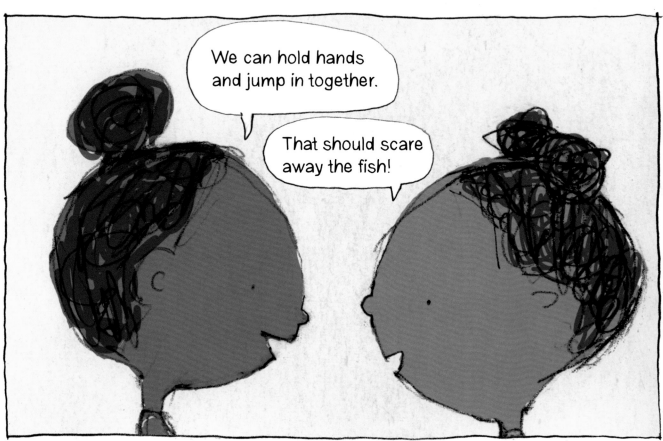

We swim

and swim

and swim.

The fish don't bite me once.

Packing up is even harder than unpacking.

When we finally get our stuff in the car,
it takes all three of us to close the boot.

It's a long drive back home.

We eat the rest of the snacks.

We stare out the window.

We stare out the window some more.

We sleep.

I think Dad missed me.

sleeping bag

sleeping mat

tent

tarpaulin

pillow

cup

mug

camp chair

bowl

dinner plate

stove

spatula

fork, spoon, knife

cooking knives

cooking spoon

mixing bowl

rope

hammer

whistle

lantern

first aid kit

coolbox

torch

binoculars

head torch

roasting fork

playing cards

pasta pot

saucepan

frying pan

paper towels

Also by Jennifer K. Mann:

ISBN: 978-1-4063-5153-8

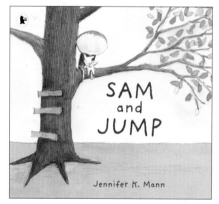

ISBN: 978-1-4063-7323-3

ISBN: 978-1-4063-8259-4

Available from all good booksellers

www.walker.co.uk